PLEASE WASH
YOUR HANDS
BEFORE YOU READ ME
AND KEEP ME CLEAN

JONATHAN and the BIG BLUE BOAT

Philip C. Stead

A NEAL PORTER BOOK

ROARING BROOK PRESS

NEW YORK

A Neal Porter Book

Published by Roaring Brook Press

Roaring Brook Press is a division of Holtzbrinck Publishing Holdings Limited Partnership

175 Fifth Avenue, New York, New York 10010

www.roaringbrookpress.com

Distributed in Canada by H. B. Fenn and Company Ltd.

Library of Congress Cataloging-in-Publication Data

Stead, Philip C.

 Jonathan and the big blue boat / Philip C. Stead. — 1st ed.

   p. cm.

 "A Neal Porter Book."

 Summary: When Jonathan's parents decide that he has gotten too old to have a stuffed animal, they trade his

favorite bear, Frederick, for a toaster, so he sets off aboard a boat, looking for Frederick.

 ISBN: 978-1-59643-562-9

 [1. Voyages and travels—Fiction. 2. Boats and boating—Fiction. 3. Teddy bears—Fiction.] I. Title.

 PZ7.S808566Jo 2011

 [E]—dc22

                    2010012952

Roaring Brook Press books are available for special promotions and premiums.

For details contact: Director of Special Markets, Holtzbrinck Publishers.

First Edition 2011

Printed in February 2011 in China by South China Printing Co. Ltd., Dongguan City, Guangdong Province

10 9 8 7 6 5 4 3 2 1

To Frederick

"It makes me feel very small," said Jonathan to Frederick. He held Frederick up high so he could see the Big Blue Boat too.

Jonathan loved the Big Blue Boat. He and Frederick would stay at the old wharf till sunset, looking up at its rusty blue hull.

One afternoon Jonathan's parents announced, "You're getting too old for a stuffed animal. So we traded your bear for a toaster." "Oh, no!" cried Jonathan. Frederick was his best friend. "Toasters really are useful," they added.

That day Jonathan walked to the old wharf alone.

"Ahoy!" called the gray-haired tugboat captain. "Why so sad?"
Jonathan sighed. "Frederick is missing. He could be anywhere
in the whole world by now."
The seagulls made a lonely sound over the harbor.
"A long time ago," said the captain, "the Big Blue Boat sailed
all over the world. My tugboat worked very hard in those days."
Standing in the shadow of the Big Blue Boat, Jonathan had
an idea.

Before long the Big Blue Boat was steaming like a tea kettle. The tugboat pulled it out past the buoys and into the open ocean. Jonathan was off to find Frederick.

"Good luck!" the captain bellowed as Jonathan waved goodbye.

And that is how Jonathan came to sail the sea on a Big Blue Boat.

A storm gathered on the high seas.
All through the night the Big Blue Boat rocked
back and forth on the tall waves.

When morning came the boat was marooned.
"Hello," said Jonathan to a mountain goat. "I'm looking for
a bear named Frederick."
The goat was startled. He had never met a sea captain before.
"I've never met a bear before," said the goat, "but
someday I would like to."
Jonathan looked up. "I could use a first mate,"
he offered, "but my boat is stuck."
The goat wagged his chin thoughtfully.
He wedged his powerful horns beneath
the boat's hull. The great ship teetered
like a seesaw and then . . .

And that is how Jonathan and a mountain goat came to sail the sea on a Big Blue Boat.

Circus tents appeared in the distance.

"Full steam ahead!" said Jonathan to the goat.

Onshore the circus was deserted except for an elephant.

"We're looking for a bear named Frederick," said Jonathan.

"I'm the only one here," the elephant replied. He lowered his trunk. "I've grown too old for the circus." The elephant looked very sad and very wise.

"We could use an experienced traveler," said Jonathan.

The Big Blue Boat began to sink.

"Oh, no!" cried the goat.

"We're shipwrecked," moaned the elephant.

"Man the lifeboats!" ordered Jonathan.

Just then, a whale swam up from under the fray, balancing the Big Blue Boat on the length of his back. He said, in a deep, slow whale voice, "The ocean can be lonely. It's good to have company."

"Pirates!" cried the elephant from the lookout perch.

"Arrr! Hand over yer treasure," ordered the pirate captain.

"We're looking for a bear named Frederick," explained Jonathan.

"They're holdin' out on us!" roared the pirate captain. "Ready the arrr-tillery! Storm the ship!"

The goat wielded his horns. The elephant stood on his hind legs, waving his tusks in the air.

"Fire!" the pirate captain yelled.

KER-BLAMMM!!!

Startled by the sound of his own cannon, the captain cried, "Retreat!"

And that is how Jonathan, a mountain goat, and a circus elephant came to sail the sea on a Big Blue Boat.

And that is how Jonathan, a mountain goat, and a circus elephant came to sail the sea on a Big Blue Boat on the back of a whale.

The elephant and goat snored like a foghorn and a
whistle, "oooоOHaaaah . . . eeeeee . . . oooоOHaaaah . . . eeeeee . . ."
Jonathan looked out at the endless sea. "Will I ever find
Frederick?" he wondered.

Far off a lighthouse blinked, showing the way to a distant port.
"Captain?" asked the whale. "Should we set a course?"

"I'll watch the ship," said the whale.

The others spent the day bear hunting in train stations and
alleyways.

They rode taxicabs and elevators and talked to pigeons along
the way. Frederick was nowhere to be found.

"Where will we look now?" asked the elephant.

A light flickered on in a shop window.

"We'll try here," said Jonathan.

Inside, the shop was cluttered but cheerful.

"Hello," said a little girl from behind the counter. In her arms she was holding . . .

"FREDERICK!" cried Jonathan.

"Oh, he's not for sale," said the little girl. "I traded a toaster for this bear. He is my best friend. I wouldn't go anywhere without him."

Jonathan smiled. After all, a big boat needs a big crew.

And that is how Jonathan, Frederick, a mountain goat, a circus elephant, and the little girl from behind the counter came to sail the sea on a Big Blue Boat on the back of a whale.